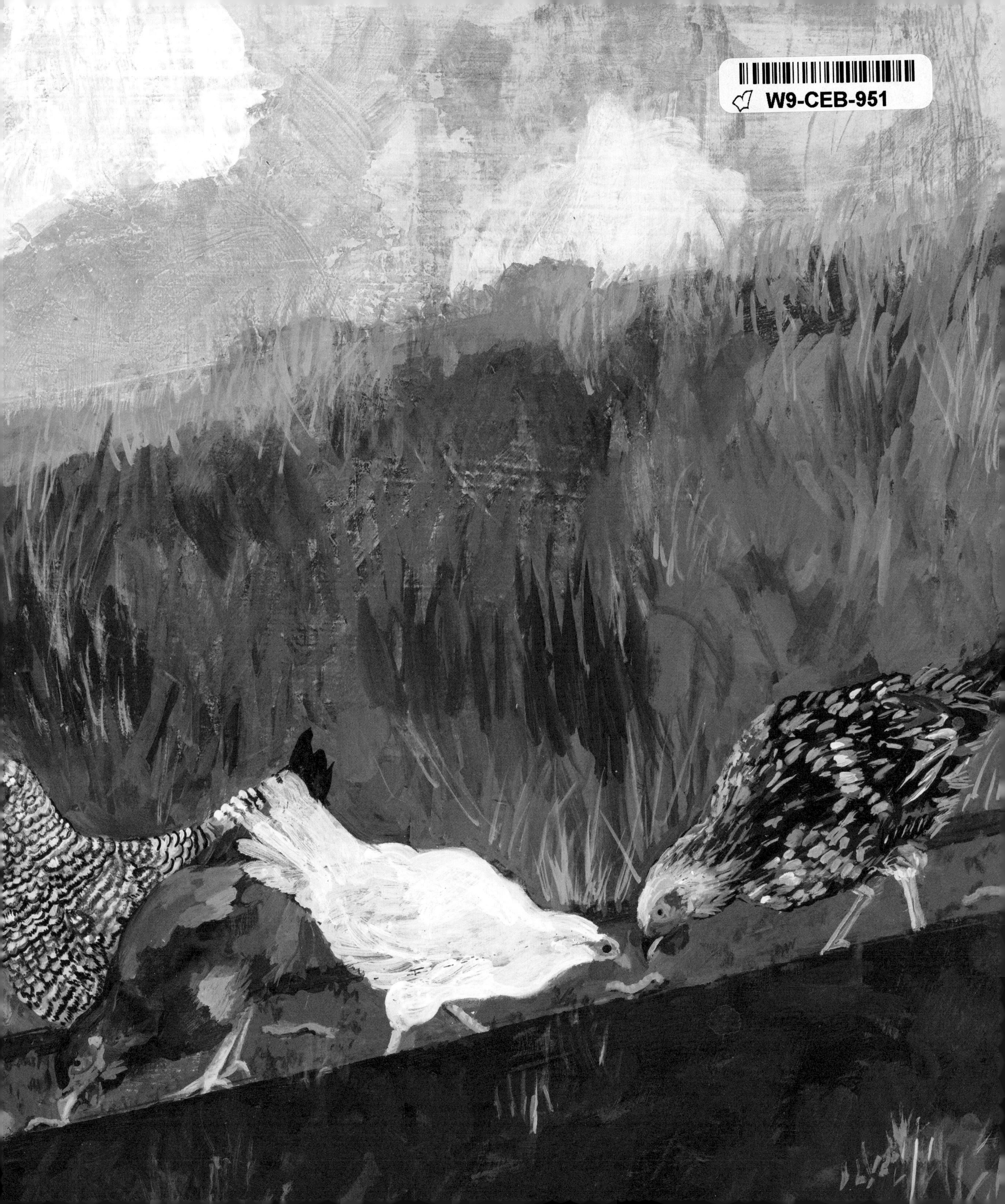

To N.A., my true heart and soul.

Many thanks to my siblings, especially Melvern, for always supporting
my writing endeavors. A heartfelt thanks to Amy Novesky, my editor,
whose critiques made this book blossom.
—M.N.

To Edna Lewis, depths seen and unseen, with love.
—C.C.

Text copyright © 2023 Melvina Noel          Illustrations copyright © 2023 Cozbi A. Cabrera

Book design by Melissa Nelson Greenberg

"Biscuits for Two or Three" from *In Pursuit of Flavor*, by Edna Lewis with Mary
Goodbody, copyright © 1988 by Edna Lewis. Used by permission of Alfred A. Knopf, an imprint
of the Knopf Doubleday Publishing Group, a division of Penguin Random House LLC. All rights reserved.

Library of Congress Cataloging-in-Publication Data available.          ISBN: 978-1-951836-39-9

Printed in China          10 9 8 7 6 5 4 3 2 1

CAMERON KIDS is an imprint of CAMERON + COMPANY

CAMERON + COMPANY
Petaluma, California
www.cameronbooks.com

# CHEF Edna

## QUEEN OF SOUTHERN COOKING, EDNA LEWIS

BY
MELVINA NOEL

ART BY
COZBI A. CABRERA

cameron kids

$\mathcal{E}$dna Regina Lewis grew up on a farm in Freetown, Virginia—
a proud African American community founded by her grandfather
and two other freed slaves.

On the farm Edna chased chickens. Milked cows. Picked wild greens.
Gathered berries.

Edna loved it all.

Especially cooking with her mother, Mama Daisy.

Spring breakfasts with fresh fish,
shad. Soaked in saltwater. Rolled
in seasoned cornmeal. Fried in
home-rendered lard.

Flavored with a slice of smoked
pork shoulder.

Summer garden vegetables. New cabbage,
potatoes, butter beans, string beans,
tomatoes, eggplant, and green corn.

Autumn harvest of root crops. Peanuts
and sweet potatoes. Field corn.

Winter fruitcakes, plum puddings,
sugar cookies, and peanut brittle.

And making biscuits.

Edna watched Mama Daisy so many
times she could make them by heart.

One. Two. Three cups of flour.
A quarter's worth of baking powder.
A dime's worth of salt.

Lard and sweet milk, thanks
to Bella, their cow.

Mixing. Kneading. Rolling. Flattening the dough.

Using an upside-down glass to
press circles. Perfect circles laid
out in rows.

Pushed into the oven, rising a mile
high. Hot and delicious biscuits.

Southern style.

And then Edna made cake.

And how did she know when her cake was done? Mama Daisy showed her how to hold her ear close to it and to listen. A bubbling sound? Back into the oven. A few minutes longer until . . . a quiet cake is done.

When Edna's father passed away, Mama Daisy and her six children had to manage grief and life.

Edna had to work to help the family.

When Edna was fifteen she left Freetown for New York.

She went to work. Ironing. Cleaning. Cooking.
Sending the money she earned back home.

Then Edna's mother passed away, and Edna worked even harder to care for her five siblings. Typing. Answering phones. Working as a seamstress. Dressing department store windows. It wasn't long before she was sought after and making clothes for movie stars.

Edna started making her own clothes, too.
Traditional African dresses. Repeating shapes
and patterns in bright, bold colors. She was so
stunning, people stopped her on New York
City streets to take her picture.

But Edna missed Freetown family and friends.

She longed for large gatherings around homemade meals. Long, white-clothed tables covered with Southern food. Warm fried chicken, thin slices of boiled Virginia ham, green beans cooked in pork stock, turnip greens picked that morning, potato salad with a boiled dressing, pickles, preserves, and yeast bread. Mincemeat, lemon meringue, and fried apple pies. Coconut and black walnut cakes. Watermelon and cantaloupe. Drinking coffee out of bowls.

Simple, pure ingredients, plus lots of love, a dash of smile, the taste of home.

Edna catered events and threw dinner parties for her new friends. Happy faces all around. Clean plates. Requests for seconds. "What kind of food is this?" they asked.

Faster than gossip, word spread about Edna's delicious Southern meals. New Yorkers wanted more Freetown food.

Soon Edna became *Chef* Edna and co-owner of a restaurant on the Upper East Side of Manhattan. Frying, roasting, stewing, baking. Roast chicken, filet mignon, fish, zucchini squash, green salad. Chocolate soufflé, caramel cake.

The restaurant was a smash. Edna peeped out from the kitchen to watch actors and editors, poets and playwrights, even a First Lady enjoy her food. It reminded her of family dinners in Freetown. One diner would beg her to make her biscuits. Another asked her if she'd studied her craft in Paris. What was her secret?

Edna just smiled. Her Paris was Freetown, the flavors of home passed down from one generation to the next.

New York, for now, was Edna's home. Union Square Greenmarket, her farm. Strolling among the stalls. Chatting with farmers. Comparing flavors. Selecting fresh fruit, vegetables, meat, and fish. Fresh, seasonal, farm-to-table ingredients for Southern cooking.

Alone in her kitchen, Edna makes biscuits again. One. Two. Three cups of flour. A quarter's worth of baking powder. A dime's worth of salt. Lard and sweet milk. Mixing. Kneading. Rolling.

She makes them all with heart.

And then Edna makes cake. She slips the batter into the oven and waits. How does she know when it's done? She holds it close, just like Mama Daisy showed her, and she listens.

A quiet cake is done.

# AUTHOR'S NOTE

While researching lesser-known African Americans who have had a positive impact on society, I learned about Edna. I am so grateful. I was drawn to her love of and impact on Southern cooking because I was also raised in the South. I enjoy cooking so much that I bought all of Edna's cookbooks! The more I read about Edna Regina Lewis, the more I wanted to know. I was so inspired that I wrote this story.

Edna was born on April 13, 1916, in Freetown, Virginia, a farming community founded by her grandfather and two of his friends shortly after their emancipation from slavery. They named the community Freetown because they wanted to be known as a town of free people. Growing up on a farm, Edna participated in all the farmwork. As a child, she learned about cooking and flavor by watching her mother prepare food in the kitchen. Her mother often baked biscuits for the men before they went out in the fields. Edna came to believe that bread should be a part of every meal.

Edna never stopped cooking. Throughout her lifetime and well into her early seventies, Edna worked as an executive chef as well as a guest chef at well-known restaurants both in and out of New York.

In addition to cooking, Edna wrote four books that focus on flavorful Southern cooking with fresh ingredients, providing not only delicious recipes and fascinating tidbits about food, but interesting stories about her life. In one of her most famous books, *In Pursuit of Flavor*, she states, "One of the greatest pleasures of my life has been that I have never stopped learning about good cooking and good food." Edna believed in the value of Southern cooking so much that she cofounded the Society for the Revival and Preservation of Southern Food.

Edna was honored with many awards, such as the James Beard Living Legend Award, the Grande Dame of Southern Cooking, and the New York Cooking Teachers' Association Cook of the Year in 1988, to name a few. In addition, she was inducted into the African American Chefs Hall of Fame, and on September 26, 2014, she was honored on a postal stamp by the United States Postal Service.

The Edna Lewis Foundation was created in January of 2012, six years after Edna passed away. Their mission statement is to "revive, preserve, and celebrate the rich history of African American cookery by cultivating a deeper understanding of Southern food and culture in America."

# EDNA'S "BISCUITS FOR TWO OR THREE"

I used to make biscuits for at least 5 or 6 people, but since I have been living alone, I have altered my biscuit recipe to make 8 or 10 large biscuits that are just the way I want them. The recipe is quick, and you do not have leftovers, which never taste as good as freshly baked biscuits. I like my biscuits large and use an upturned glass or empty 2½-inch-round tin can to stamp them out. If I know I will be making these or any other biscuits, I measure everything out beforehand, and then all I have to do is mix the dough and bake the biscuits.

MAKES 8 TO 10 BISCUITS
½ pound unbleached all-purpose flour
½ teaspoon salt
4 teaspoons single-acting baking powder
2 ounces chilled lard
⅔ cup milk

Put the flour, salt, baking powder, and lard in a mixing bowl. Blend with a pastry blender or with your fingertips until the mixture is the texture of cornmeal. Add the milk all at once and stir the mixture well with a stout spoon. Scrape the dough out of the bowl onto a lightly floured surface. Sprinkle the dough lightly with 1 teaspoon of flour to prevent its sticking to your fingers. Knead the dough for a few seconds and shape it into a round, thick cake. Dust the rolling surface and the rolling pin again lightly with flour and roll the dough from the center outward into a circle. Lift up the dough and turn it as you roll to make a circle 9 inches in diameter. Pierce the dough all over with a dinner fork and cut with a biscuit cutter, beginning on the outer edge and cutting in as close as possible to avoid too much leftover dough. This will yield 8 to 10 large biscuits. Place on a heavy cookie sheet or baking pan. Bake in preheated 450°F oven for 12 to 13 minutes. Remove from the oven and allow to cool for 3 or 4 minutes before serving. Serve hot. Biscuits can be warmed over successfully if set uncovered in a hot oven for no more than 4 to 5 minutes.

# SELECT SOURCES

Franklin, Sara B., ed. *Edna Lewis: At the Table with an American Original.* Chapel Hill: University of North Carolina Press, 2018.

Lam, Francis. "Edna Lewis and the Black Roots of American Cooking." *New York Times Magazine,* October 28, 2015.

Lewis, Edna. *In Pursuit of Flavor.* Charlottesville, VA: University Press of Virginia, 1988.

Lewis, Edna. *The Taste of Country Cooking.* New York: Alfred A. Knopf, 2018.

Lewis, Edna, and Evangeline Peterson. *The Edna Lewis Cookbook.* Edinburg, VA: Axios Press, 1972.

Barash, Bailey, dir. *Fried Chicken and Sweet Potato Pie.* 2005. Atlanta, GA: Bbarash Productions, 2005. http://www.snagfilms.com/films/title/fried_chicken_and_sweet_potato_pie.

To learn more about Edna, visit the Edna Lewis Foundation: ednalewisfoundation.org.